Ants

by Saviana Stanescu

A SAMUEL FRENCH ACTING EDITION

SAMUEL FRENCH
FOUNDED 1830

SAMUELFRENCH.COM
SAMUELFRENCH-LONDON.CO.UK

FOR PRODUCTION ENQUIRIES

UNITED STATES AND CANADA
Info@SamuelFrench.com
1-866-598-8449

UNITED KINGDOM AND EUROPE
Plays@SamuelFrench-London.co.uk
020-7255-4302

Each title is subject to availability from Samuel French, depending upon country of performance. Please be aware that *ANTS* may not be licensed by Samuel French in your territory. Professional and amateur producers should contact the nearest Samuel French office or licensing partner to verify availability.

MUSIC USE NOTE

IMPORTANT BILLING AND CREDIT REQUIREMENTS

ANTS was first produced by the New Jersey Repertory Company, February 7 - March 10, 2013. The performance was directed by Jeff Zinn, with sets by Jessica Parks, costumes by Patricia E. Doherty, lighting design by Jill Nagle, sound design by Merek Royce Press, technical director Michael "Rusty" Carroll. The Production Stage Manager was Jennifer Tardibuono. The cast was as follows:

MIA	. . . . Maria Silverman
ADAM	. . . . Michael Samuel Kaplan
KARA	. . . . Carol Todd

The play was written and developed at the Lark Play Development Center, Playground Program, where an additional round table was directed by Daniella Topol. In 2010, a workshop and public reading was held at the Ensemble Studio Theatre, also directed by Daniella Topol. The cast was as follows:

MIA	. . . . Polly Lee
ADAM	. . . . Robert Montano
KARA	. . . . Maria Striar

In 2012, a workshop and public reading was held at The New Group. The performance was directed by Ian Morgan. The cast was as follows:

MIA	. . . . Sofia Gomez
ADAM	. . . . Steven Rishard
KARA	. . . . Carol Todd

CHARACTERS

KARA – late 30s, attractive, speaks with an accent (any race or ethnicity)

MIA – Kara's younger sister, 29, boyish, speaks with a strong accent (same race/ethnicity as Kara)

DR. ADAM KOHN – Professor of Biochemistry, 48, speaks with a mild accent (any race or ethnicity)

SETTING

A small American town and a University in the same area.
Maybe CT.

TIME

2009 – The Chinese Year of the Ox
and the American Year of the Recession.

NOTES

A / signifies the point of overlapping dialogue.

1.

*(Spotlight on **MIA** - downstage, addressing the audience.)*

(She constructs her speech carefully, paying attention to her newly found sophistication with the English language. It's intense and weirdly funny.)

MIA. Ants. They never get tired. They never stop. I could watch them forever. Unfortunately, I do get tired sometimes. All those inconveniences of being human: eat, sleep, talk, socialize. I don't socialize much but still. I need 9 hours of sleep daily. I'm below a worker-ant. But I am bigger. In the ants world, I would be a QUEEN. Everybody would work for me. All I'd have to do is reproduce. Kinda boring. Whadda fuck?! - as the Americans put it. Where is your scientific tone?

(composure, scientific tone)

All societies are characterized by struggles for control: which individuals gain the spoils and which toil in the fields. In colonies of social insects this struggle is embodied by a reproductive division of labor. Some individuals (the queens) reproduce, while the workers provide the labor that maintains colony function. The queens are bigger and can live for up to 30 years while workers live from 1 to 3 years. Totally unfair. How is it determined which individuals, as developing larvae, are becoming QUEENS or different types of WORKERS? It is largely based on the NUTRITION they receive. Nutritional and genetic factors contribute in different ways to how big an individual grows... *(change of tone)* Think big! The Nobel Prize. I want to win the Nobel Prize. I'll be the first one from my country to win it. It's gonna take 15-20 years... Ten generations of worker ants. But this is the good part of being human: we live longer than the ants. But less than the sea turtles.

Anyway. Focus! Americans win Nobel Prizes all the time. But now I am here too. America nurtures me.

(KARA enters.)

KARA. Are you talking to the walls again?

MIA. I'm talking to people. Imaginary people.

(KARA turns the lights on: the living room of their house. KARA holds a few envelopes.)

KARA. In darkness? You can't "see" imaginary people with the lights on?

MIA. I can't focus with the lights on. I suck at lecturing in English, I suck, I suck, / I suck...

KARA. You can't suck, we speak only English in this house. So you can – how did you put it? – be immersed in English. "Swim" in English. Breathe in English. Dream in English.

MIA. Would you please let me continue my lecture?

KARA. *(ironically)* Oh, excuse my silly interruption, "professor"! I'm honored to have you around. May I humbly ask what is this lecture for? Did you get a teaching job?

MIA. No, it's for a conference.

KARA. A conference? Are they paying you to go?

MIA. A future conference. A possible conference. I must be prepared.

KARA. Of course. An imaginary conference.

MIA. *(half-joking)* For when I get the Nobel Prize.

KARA. Right. And I get the Oscar. Until then we've got these...

(KARA waves the envelopes at her.)

MIA. *(teasing)* Letters from your fans?

KARA. Bills - my most faithful fans. You wanna pay them? You're more than welcome. Please, help yourself. Pick one. Gas, Electricity, Cable...

MIA. *(steps away from the bills)* More bills? Already?

KARA. Like you ever notice a month passing. Yes, bills, bills, bills. Fuck them.

(She throws them in the garbage.)

MIA. You don't open them?

KARA. I know what's in there. Mortgage, Gas, Electricity, Cable and TV, my cell phone, YOUR cell phone, YOUR student loan...

MIA. But we need to pay them.

KARA. That's a very profound statement, Mia. Yes, WE do. So you better get a job because... I'm... I can't... I just... I got fired.

MIA. It's a joke, isn't it?

KARA. Yeah, my best joke ever. Joking my life here.

MIA. You mean you really... But you've been working in this factory for like 17 years. You're a good worker. What did your boss say? Why – why you? You said he liked you. He parked his car next to yours all the time so he could talk with you after / program.

KARA. The economy is bad, blah, blah. We all must tighten the belt, make sacrifices, the factory is not working full capacity, the automobile industry is having a hard time so we too, cuz we are supplying for them, blah, blah, something like that. Oh, and he said: you're attractive, you're still young, you'll find something better. I always thought you could do better than this factory, so take this opportunity to advance your goals and your self-esteem. And he kissed me on my cheek. Moron. Selfish moron.

MIA. He's right, you can advance your goals.

KARA. My goals... Wait to hear more. Bad news comes in avalanches...

MIA. Nothing can be totally bad. Our old proverb: a kick in the ass is a step forward!? You'll find another job, a better one, where you can really express yourself. Your boss did you a BIG favor!

KARA. Oh, shut up!

MIA. We'll start thinking of a new job for you, an exciting one.

KARA. Too bad... I was kinda thinking to float on your back for a while...

MIA. "Float on your back"? I don't know this expression. You mean swim backwards?

KARA. No, I mean: YOU get a job, I stay home for a while. Figure things out. Give myself Tarot readings. Ask the universe for a truce. Then for a direction.

(**KARA** *takes the bills out of the garbage can and hands them to* **MIA.**)

KARA. They're yours, baby sis. You're the head of the family now.

MIA. OK, you're going to "float on my back"... We have to maintain control of this situation.

(**KARA** *nods. She looks a little pale and sick, but she starts walking around the living room, stopping from time to time to move an object (a vase, a pen, a magazine – anything) 1-2 inches left or right.*)

(**MIA**, *unopened bills in her hand, follows* **KARA** *with her eyes, like studying a trapped animal.*)

KARA. Did you eat?

MIA. No. I waited for you.

KARA. Did you cook anything?

MIA. I had to do some work, the research / on -

KARA. I know, busy busy bee, taking care of your cockroaches, your rats -

MIA. Ants.

KARA. *(pacing the room)* Rats, ants, whatever.

MIA. Take a seat, why are you wandering around like a drunken fly?

KARA. Oh, yeah, believe me: I'd love to drink my brains out and fly away to... China. Antarctica. New Zealand. New... London. No, that's too close. New... Jersey. New-fucking-something. New York!

MIA. Are you depressed?

KARA. When someone is sad or mad or, I dunno, just sick of life, you scientists call it "depression". You give us pills and send us to the shrink. Like everything can be solved with a pill.

MIA. It can, most of the time.

KARA. OK, OK, Miss Know-it-all, Miss PhD in Biology. I'm too tired / to argue -

MIA. Biochemistry.

KARA. Right. Bio-fuckin'-chemistry. Does it bring any money? Noooo. What a blasphemy to ask!

MIA. I'm applying for a few fellowships.

KARA. *(sinking into a chair)* God knows how difficult it was for me to pay for your master, Mia. Now this PhD thing… You don't need a PhD to teach in public schools. They need teachers and your English is good enough.

MIA. Why are you talking like this? I thought you understood. I am working on a revolutionary theory that will change our perception on ant colonies, / it will -

KARA. Fuck the ants! Think about people for a minute. Ants are just little… ugly, small, boring, harmful … too many.

MIA. *(morosely)* What are you saying – I should give up?

KARA. You don't need that PhD. You're already over-educated.

MIA. I should be a… loser… who can't finish what she started?

KARA. Never mind. You only have one more year and you're done. You'll be done, won't you?

MIA. I'll be an ABD.

KARA. What's that?

MIA. All but dissertation.

KARA. And you'll get a job. A real job. A teaching job in a university.

MIA. Maybe. I hope so anyway.

KARA. That professor of yours must help.

MIA. Adam? He will give me a recommendation, of course.

(**MIA** *sits on the sofa. She puts the unopened bills on the coffee table.*)

KARA. He must give you more than that. He must hire you. He promised he would let you teach. He did. You told me so.

MIA. I'll have a course to teach next semester, but it's not like he's gonna hire me full-time. I'll have to be an adjunct for a few years. You don't know how things work in academia.

KARA. A few years? But you must get a job, Mia, you must. You're becoming one of those things of yours, the male-bee-parasite, and you're not even a male, you're a girl, you should have a boyfriend, marry a nice American man, solve all our problems.

MIA. Why haven't you married a nice American man and solved all our problems?

KARA. I came here alone, with no English. I had to rely on a stable salary. To send money home. To YOU. I had to work. In a factory. Assembly line... Do you know what an assembly line is? You're there with 80 others, same faces, same gestures... you try to think of something nice, or clever, or sexy, or imaginative. But you can't. Your brain shuts off. You become one of those little metal pieces.

MIA. Your brain shuts off only when you're dead.

KARA. Then what do you call this: alarm, shower, coffee, boiled egg, car, factory, work, work, lunch break – breathe for a moment – work, work, car, back home, shower, dinner, TAROT, TV, bed, sleep. Did I have any time to date? And what is dating anyway – another routine. True love, passion, have disappeared from our lives. This is a world for robots, not for people... You better create clones in your freakin' lab, adult human-clones who have no desire to laugh, to love, to play... This is not a world for children...

MIA. You got laid off. It's not the end of the world. *(trying to joke)* You'll meet a charming Cockroach Prince riding his golden winged rat, and you'll be happy / ever after.

KARA. Stop those silly biology-jokes, Mia! They make me puke. Literally.

MIA. You're being overdramatic.

KARA. I'm being… pregnant!

MIA. Pregnant?!

KARA. Pregnant.

MIA. Like… with baby-to-be?

KARA. Like freakin' pregnant! Do you need a dictionary?

MIA. Wow. We're deep in… soap-opera.

KARA. That's all you have to say?

MIA. What about the classical: Who's the father?

KARA. It doesn't matter. He's married.

MIA. He can still recognize the child. Is he… your boss?

KARA. God, no.

MIA. Someone from work? He must pay child support. I know that much.

KARA. It won't be any child. I can't afford it.

MIA. Oh, no. Here I have something to say. Your mom instinct will kick in. We'll have a baby in the house! She's gonna be so much fun and / we'll buy her little toys and -

KARA. We can't afford her or him. I lost my job, remember.

MIA. Don't you worry! I'll find something. I'll work at the library, at the admissions office, at the… suicide hotline, anything.

KARA. It's not gonna be enough… we're talking 3500 a month for just the two of us, without the little one. No. I can't afford it.

MIA. Wait! Please wait a few days, a week, two weeks. You'll see, I'll find something.

KARA. You'll need a full-time job. You won't have time for your research.

MIA. I'll find a solution. You don't need to work anymore. You're a queen now. Sit down. Please, we need to take care of the little Pupa.

KARA. Pupa?!

MIA. Baby-ant.

KARA. OK, Mia… It's useless to talk to you. *(beat)* I'm starving. I gotta cook something. Pilaf or mashed potatoes?

MIA. I'll cook. Don't you move.

(She's ready to go to the kitchen.)

KARA. I'm not just gonna sit here and ... I'm not a cripple. *(She stands up.)*

MIA. Do your TAROT, read your horoscopes. See what's gonna be pupa's sign.

KARA. Stop call it "pupa"!

MIA. I like it better than "larva".

KARA. Shut up. Go read your books, I'll cook.

MIA. I have a question though: if you didn't want a child, why didn't you just use some… you know… contraceptives?

KARA. Is that what life is? A pack of pills, a YES-NO form, an assembly line with clearly defined questions and answers... *(beat)* I guess I cheated a bit. Maybe I wanted a child but I didn't want to admit it. Or maybe I just wanted to let things happen naturally. To be surprised. To see what questions the universe sends towards me. To open my body to that question and try to answer it.

(KARA feels unexpectedly dizzy and sits on the sofa.)

MIA. See? You have to rest now. (KARA *nods, looking surprised by her need to just sit.*)

KARA. We have pastas, cheese, sour cream. You can make spaghetti carbonara, it's easy.

MIA. I'll make the best spaghetti of your life, my queen!

(MIA walks downstage and addresses the audience.)

2.

MIA. Ants develop through a complete life cycle of egg, larva, pupa, and adult. The egg is tiny, almost microscopic in size. The larva is legless and grub-like, very soft and whitish in color. It is also helpless and depends totally on workers for food and care. The pupa looks somewhat like the adult but is soft, unpigmented, and cannot move around. Some are enclosed in a cocoon, some are not. A newly-emerged adult requires several days for its body to harden and darken. *(change of tone)* I didn't realize Kara was so unhappy. Back home, everybody envies her: she's THE American. She has a nice house, a job... Well, now she lost her job. We'll find something. Pupa must have everything she needs. She will be big and strong, smart and happy. She's on to a good start. She's an American citizen. And she has me around. If I need to turn into a worker-ant for her, I will, I'm telling you, I will.

3.

(The Biochemistry Lab at the University. A microphone/ recorder, a computer, etc.)

(ADAM and MIA work together, looking from time to time through a microscope, making notes, recording some observations.)

ADAM. *(into the microphone)* In the ant Aphaenogaster cockerelli, we mimicked reproductive cheaters by applying a synthetic compound typical of fertile individuals on nonreproductive workers.

MIA. *(in low voice)* We framed these poor non-reproductive worker-ants...

ADAM. *(into the microphone)* This treatment induced nestmate aggression in colonies where a queen was present. This provides the first direct evidence that cuticular hydrocarbons are the informational basis of policing behaviors, serving a major function in the regulation of reproduction in social insects.

(He gestures to MIA to record her observations.)

MIA. *(into the microphone)* Some ant species are known not only to attack cheating workers, but also to destroy their eggs.

ADAM. *(to MIA)* That's another issue. Focus on THIS experiment. *(into the microphone)* Cheaters are identified through information that is inherently reliable.

MIA. It's not fair!

ADAM. "Some ant species" is not reliable info, you must be very specific in these recordings.

MIA. No, it's unfair for the ants! What we did. Make them seem reproductive cheaters when they are honest workers. I mean they're getting attacked because of us... And they're not even trying to reproduce...

ADAM. Do you have a question here? I don't really see where are you going with this. We've been working on this project for a year now, you're saying you don't consider it anymore for your dissertation?

MIA. I actually have a… an ethical question.

ADAM. An ethical question? Shoot.

MIA. *(into the microphone)* We applied a synthetic compound typical of fertile individuals to non-reproductive worker ants. We basically framed them. Is that OK, ethically speaking?

ADAM. *(stopping the recording)* Mia! You knew very well what we were doing here when you joined our research team on "reproductive policing in ants colonies".

MIA. Yes, but… We can at least help those ants we framed, now that we've seen they were attacked / and -

ADAM. Help them? How do you suggest to help them? We can't make them queens. It's too late. They don't correspond genetically. They are too small.

MIA. We can help them have "babies".

ADAM. What are we – a fertility clinic?

MIA. It's just fair to allow them now their… little thing. The parthenogenesis.

ADAM. You must be tired. Take 10 and bring me a veggie sandwich from the cafeteria.

Warm it up a bit. I hate frozen veggies. This is the only thing I couldn't get used to in America: ice in beverages and cold veggies. And I've been here for 24 years now. 25 in August… Bring me a large coffee too! Milk, no sugar, as always. OK, go now, we have to start the new series of tests.

MIA. But, Adam…

ADAM. But-but-but. We are scientists. There's no "but" in science, just "butt".

(He slaps her ass playfully.)

Go.

MIA. You're not allowed to do that. That's very… sexist.

ADAM. Yeah, yeah, you're right, I won't do it with the American girls, they'd sue me. But you won't do that, will you? You were raised differently. In our countries, it wasn't such a big deal to be playful with a woman. It's fun to flirt a bit. It relieves the tension accumulated during work hours. Nothing is more energy-boosting than a pretty woman's scent when she flirts back.

MIA. But I wasn't flirting with you.

ADAM. "But" again? You must be a little more disciplined if you want that course next semester.

MIA. I actually need a full-time job.

ADAM. A full-time job? That's hard to get. But not impossible for a smart girl like you. Go. I and the ants will wait for you. *(joking)* We won't reproduce without you.

(**MIA** *walks downstage.*)

4.

*(**MIA** addresses the audience.)*

MIA. The worker ants are biologically capable of a type of <u>parthenogenesis,</u> the process that allows a female to produce offspring without a mate. When they try, however, they produce chemicals called <u>pheromones</u> that their sisters detect with antennas.

It's basically smell, but not really the smell we humans know. More of a scent. A horny ant's scent.

If the colony lacks a queen, workers are permitted to have their own babies. But when a queen is present, only she is allowed to produce the pheromone that signals fertility status. If a worker tries to "cheat," her sisters will physically restrain the disobedient ant from successfully reproducing. Of course, it was important to figure out how they discover the cheaters. But, but, but – enough is enough, we should stop framing those poor ants. *(beat)* It would be much more interesting if we could make them queens. Now, that would be a true revolution in science. Revolution and evolution...

Yes, that's it, from theory to practice: I'll make the worker-ants queens. And I'll get a full-time position, a biiiiig award, a faaaaat fellowship, something!

5.

(A motel room, lunchtime.)

*(**ADAM** is getting dressed, **KARA** is still in bed.)*

KARA. The advantage of being unemployed: I don't have to rush to get dressed anymore. I don't have a lunch break anymore. I only have a long stressful unlimited break.

ADAM. You should do something about getting a new job, Kara. I can't hire Mia full-time. Impossible.

KARA. But you must.

ADAM. Must? May I remind you that you're not my... boss.

KARA. If my daddy were the president of the University, you'd lick my toes and sign whatever paper I put in front of you...

ADAM. Leave my wife out of this.

KARA. Sure, leave the "queen of coins" out of this. It's not like I have four kids like her. Two with you, one adopted, one with her first husband – / the lawyer...

ADAM. We agreed not to talk about her.

KARA. And of course I'm not 12 years older than you. To tell you what you "must" do. Didn't she just turn 60?

ADAM. Enough, Kara. Beth is a beautiful person, a wonderful mother, and wife.

KARA. Sure, gimme the positive bullshit speech! You married her for the American citizenship, c'mon, admit it, it's time for you to admit it!

ADAM. I think I was clear with you from the very beginning. I told you I wouldn't leave my family / for this little -

KARA. Yes, yes, you were very clear. Just sex, no feelings.

ADAM. I didn't say "no feelings"...

KARA. What did you tell... Beth? Just marriage, no sex after 55?

ADAM. It's only natural to lose the excitement after 25 years.

KARA. Natural selection – that's how Mia would call it, all this family-dance to get ahead.

(**KARA** *gets out of the bed, wrapping the sheet around her body.*)

ADAM. I'm not going to get angry. You can say whatever you want. You are particularly bitter today. Even bitchy. I understand, you got laid off. It's not easy. I'll do whatever I can to help.

KARA. Give Mia a full-time teaching position.

ADAM. I can't do that. She doesn't have her PhD yet. She's not even an ABD.

KARA. You are the Chair of the department, you can do whatever you want.

ADAM. Things don't work like this here, Kara. Back in the old countries, each boss was a little dictator, he could do whatever he wanted: fuck all the pretty employees, hire virgins and fuck them, fire the husbands of the women he wanted to fuck, fuck everybody up and down, left and right. Power, they had power, those bastards. Had I stayed there… I might have become one of them. But I'm not there, Kara, I'm here, we are in America, and there are rules here, that's why it's called democracy.

KARA. Blah, blah, blah. *(beat)* What if I was pregnant, what then?

ADAM. You're saying you don't take any pills?

KARA. I hate pills. I like things… natural.

ADAM. You should have told me that.

KARA. I'm telling you now.

ADAM. Well, if you are pregnant – but there are 98% chances that you are not as you haven't gotten pregnant in the last 5 years – however, in the hypothesis of an unwanted pregnancy…

(she looks at him: "unwanted"?)

There are a few solutions: adoption, single-motherhood, abortion… or… I could take the child,

I'm sure Beth wouldn't say no. She's really a generous person. We have a big house, we're not poor... see "the devil is not so dark" as we used to say in the old country.

KARA. Fuck you! I won't give her my child.

ADAM. You started all this "let's have a little tragedy" game. Relax. You're not pregnant.

KARA. How do you know? Is that a scientifically proven fact?

ADAM. Let's say, I don't "smell" any pregnancy.

KARA. Wow, doctor. That's good.

ADAM. I gotta go now. I have a faculty meeting at 2 pm.

KARA. Sure. Good luck.

ADAM. Shall I reserve this room for next week?

KARA. I dunno. I don't think so.

ADAM. I don't have time for games, Kara.

KARA. It's not a game. It's just... I don't "smell" any future for us.

ADAM. OK. You're in a bad mood. It's understandable. I'll call you on Monday.

KARA. Don't call me anymore.

ADAM. *(about to leave the room)* You'll feel better next week, you'll see.

KARA. Give my coldest regards to your "queen".

(He leaves.)

6.

MIA. <u>A queen</u> is generally the largest individual in the colony. She has wings until after her mating flight, when she removes them. <u>The workers</u> are sterile, wingless females who build and repair the nest, care for the brood, defend the nest, and feed both immature and adult ants, including the queen. *(change of tone)* Here's my big plan: I'm gonna transform those poor wingless worker-ants we framed as reproductive cheaters into QUEENS. I'm gonna develop a synthetic compound that will make them "smell" like Queens. At least for a while. Until they reproduce. And their eggs automatically become queen's eggs. *(beat)*

I'll dedicate my life to finding a compound that makes them queens for life, that's irreversible. This is gonna be my big discovery! I can "smell" the Nobel Prize. For turning workers into queens. For giving them WINGS.

7.

(The living room of **KARA***'s and* **MIA***'s house.* **KARA** *gives herself a Tarot reading.)*

KARA. *(reading the cards as she turns them)* In the Self position: Ten of swords. You're feeling the taste of dust. You've been defeated. That's nothing you can do and it's appropriate to admit it. All right, I admit it. In the Situation position: Wheel of Fortune. You never know what's gonna come. Sometimes you are up, sometimes you are down. Get used to it, ride the wheel with composure. OK. Compose yourself... Four of coins in the Challenges position. Poverty consciousness... Right. Nothing new here.

*(**MIA** enters, throwing her bag on the sofa.)*

MIA. Hey.

KARA. Hey.

MIA. What are the cards saying?

KARA. Same old shit: we are poor and aware of it. How was your day? Any news on the job front?

MIA. I went to the Library, to Career Services, to the IT labs, the Campus Administration, the Suicide Hotline, but... *(beat)* It's because I'm a foreign student, I can't get hired even in the admissions office or cafeteria without a green card, can you believe that?

KARA. What's not to believe.

MIA. I can't be "work-study". Which means I can't really work there, except for research and grants that I could get for my research. And teaching of course, but that's a long shot. It sucks! *(beat)* Anyway, they pay so little – like ten bucks an hour. You work eight hours, the whole day, and you can only buy like what: two books. A waste of time. I can do a lot in those eight hours. I can progress my research. This shitty work situation actually motivates me to focus fully on my research. Time is important, time is progress. *(beat)*

Why don't you say anything?

KARA. I dunno. I guess I'm... paralyzed, I'm just... I dunno.

MIA. What are we gonna do? How much do you have in savings?

KARA. There are four families on our street going through foreclosures, or even more, but they are hiding it... Rich people don't like to admit they got poor, for them it's even worse than for us, they're used to having money... We can lose the house.

MIA. You don't have any savings.

KARA. I have about... 4000 dollars. Enough for a month of living, and an abortion.

MIA. No, no... That's not an option.

KARA. It's a necessity.

MIA. But we want a child!

KARA. I don't want it. And I don't wanna talk about it anymore. (*She walks to the window. She wants to avoid the painful topics.*) We need a brighter light in the courtyard.

MIA. What? Oh, yeah. A 100 Watts bulb will do it. That one is a 40.

KARA. (*beat*) The Year of the Ox is said to bring good fortune and prosperity. I guess that's not for us, not for Goats and Rats.

MIA. I thought I was a Tiger in the Chinese horoscope.

KARA. You wish. You're a Goat and I'm a Rat. (*beat*) Your professor is an Ox. This year is gonna be good for him. His wife is an Ox too. Two prosperous Oxen. Good for them.

MIA. How do you know when Adam was born?

KARA. You mentioned he was 48.

MIA. I don't think I did.

KARA. You did. You told me he was 48 and all the gossip about his old fat wife.

MIA. I didn't say she was fat. I've never seen her.

KARA. I know some people who knew him since he came to this country. He changed his name, he cut the last part... he wanted so much to be an American. That's why he married her. Kohn is actually Kohnashevsky..., Kohnjevich, Kohnagamba, something like that.

MIA. You just found out about all that?

KARA. I've known it for years.

MIA. You never mentioned it.

KARA. I wanted you to respect him. He's your boss.

MIA. My professor and my thesis advisor, not my boss.

(Silence.)

KARA. He must give you a teaching position or a grant.

MIA. Why don't you ask the father of the baby to help? That would make much more sense. He impregnated / you.

KARA. He wants to take my baby and raise it with his wife. That's not gonna happen. I'd rather kill him. The baby.

MIA. No! We will take care of her. Or him. But the father must pay.

KARA. *(outburst)* When is that Adam gonna really do something for us!?

*(Pause. **MIA**'s revelation.)*

MIA. It's his... It's Adam's...

KARA. I'm sorry, Mia, I should have... Anyway. Better to have everything out in the open.

MIA. Since when have you two...

KARA. Five years. More or less.

MIA. It sucks...

KARA. That's how we got you here. He wrote the support letter for your student visa.

*(Silence. **MIA** takes it in.)*

MIA. No, I got accepted into the program based on my own merits.

KARA. Of course. He wouldn't have accepted you otherwise. But he was able to accept you instead of other foreign students. The places were limited.

MIA. He liked my paper. He said it was "revolutionary". He really liked my work!

KARA. He did.

MIA. No, I didn't get in because of you, or him, or because you and him, I got in because I'm good! I'm good!

KARA. Of course you're good.

MIA. I need to go out, I need… beer, whisky, something, anything.

KARA. But you don't drink, Mia.

*(**MIA** puts a jacket on.)*

MIA. *(heading out)* I'm going to the campus. It's a party there.

KARA. You never go to those parties! Mia! We need to talk, to make some decisions, we are in a shitty situation, / we…

MIA. It's not WE. YOU are in a shitty situation and dragged me down with you. You want to drown both of us. You can't stand swimming alone in your own DO-IT-YOURSELF shit.

(She leaves, slamming the door.)

KARA. Mia! Wait!

MIA. *(off stage)* Where did you put my bike?!

KARA. In the fuckin' garage!

8.

(A party on the campus. **MIA** *still has her helmet on.)*

MIA. *(to a male student off stage)* Fuck off, that wasn't a kiss, it was a stupid exchange of saliva and I DIDN'T LIKE IT! Nerd!

(She gets outside, drinking a beer. Party music can be heard in the background.)

Male ants are generally winged and keep their wings until death. The male ant's only function is to mate with the queen. Once he does, he dies, generally within two weeks.

(pause, drinking)

Adam Kohn, you are dead! I'm gonna cut cut cut your wings! You don't deserve them, bastard! You have a wife, why did you have to fuck around with my sister? *(drinking)* It's not that I don't like you, I do, I would have liked you as a brother-in-law, I would. But guess what, you are married, stupid! *(pause, drinking)*

That wife of yours, she has it all, hasn't she? She's the real Queen. She has kids, she has money, she has a house. She has you. What do we have? Me and my sister – we have nothing. We have a mortgage and routines and worries and debt. My sister hasn't had a real vacation in 17 years! 17 years of summers in that freakin' factory while you and your wife – and your kids – were laying in the sun in Cancun or... fucking Jamaica. I hate you, Adam Kohn. I hate you!!!

9.

(The Biochemistry Lab.)

*(**MIA** is standing, **ADAM** is sitting.)*

ADAM. OK. What is so important that it couldn't wait? That you didn't prepare the synthetic hydrocarbon?

MIA. I know about you and my sister.

ADAM. Oh, that. That shouldn't interfere with our work here.

MIA. You must help your baby.

ADAM. What baby are you talking about?

MIA. Kara is pregnant. With you. Do you deny that?

ADAM. Wait a minute. This is a strategy to show me that framing non-reproductive ants as cheaters is wrong. I got your point. No need for this new soap-opera. We are not in Hollywood here.

MIA. So you don't want to admit it's your child.

ADAM. Mia, it's not OK to do such things to your professor. Your thesis advisor. I was planning to help you guys, but now…

MIA. But, but, but… now I found out that you cheated on your wife with my sister. That you got her pregnant. We are … family now. Her baby is your child and my niece. Or nephew. We both have some responsibility in all this.

ADAM. So this is serious. She's really pregnant?

MIA. Yeah, she pukes like every five minutes. You don't wanna be in our home now. We are facing foreclosure she lost her job, we are in a kinda… desperate situation.

ADAM. Well. This is quite some news.

MIA. So I need you to do two things.

ADAM. I can take care of the baby. I already told that to Kara.

MIA. Liar. You said you didn't know.

ADAM. She presented me with the hypothesis, not the fact.

MIA. We don't want to give the baby to you and your wife. We want 4000 dollars each month, as child support, and we won't even tell your wife. And I want something else too.

ADAM. You are not in the position to negotiate with me.

MIA. I'm not negotiating with you. I'm telling you what's what.

ADAM. Don't piss me off, I want to find a way to support you guys, but / if you piss me off -

MIA. You will do what I'm telling you to do. And more.

ADAM. *(standing up)* This is ridiculous.

MIA. I wrote a sexual harassment complaint. Tomorrow it is going to the dean.

ADAM. What?! You don't have any reasons to complain. I didn't do anything to you. Except slap your ass once or twice. That's not sexual harassment.

MIA. I took the liberty to add some stuff. A "synthetic compound". I said you forced me to give you a blowjob.

ADAM. *(amused)* That's crazy. Nobody will believe you. *(seriously)* I have a certain prestige in this school, why would anyone believe you?

MIA. Because Mary Segal and Megan Kartis accused you of sexual harassment six years ago and you managed to come out clean, to get pushed back in business by your father-in-law, the President of the University. But, but, but – that can't happen again because he retired last year. I did my research.

(Silence. Finally **ADAM** *takes the whole situation in.)*

ADAM. What do you actually want?

MIA. 4000 dollars each month – baby support.

(Pause. They look at each other.)

ADAM. OK.

MIA. And you won't take the baby.

ADAM. That's fine. Perfect. I don't really need a new born. I have grown up children. *(beat)*

So this is it. I'll take 10 to calm myself. *(beat)* Do you want a coffee or anything from the cafeteria?

MIA. I'm not done yet.

ADAM. I won't slap your ass anymore, I won't touch you or your sister ever in my life. I swear to God. You're troublemakers.

MIA. Great. But now comes what I really want, for myself I mean. The other stuff was for Kara.

ADAM. Shoot.

MIA. We stop the experiment, we won't frame the ants as reproductive cheaters anymore. We will create a new compound that makes them seem queens to the other ants, so they can grow wings and reproduce as they please. This is my final condition.

ADAM. Now this is really silly. We can't interfere in the life of the ant colony in that way. We can't create queens. It would be an elaborate and useless process – why would we want to do that?

MIA. Because we can.

ADAM. This is the most fantasist idea I've ever heard.

MIA. It's not negotiable. The sexual harassment complaint is my most convincing piece of writing ever.

ADAM. Do you realize what you're asking me? To stop the experiment we got funding from the Einstein Foundation for and start something else, a completely ridiculous something else… a sort of high school utopia… a simplistic nonsense… a useless aberration…

MIA. You can "frame" the topic in a clever way so that we can still get funding. You've done it before. You thought I didn't notice? I'm not stupid.

ADAM. You're not stupid, I give you that. You're just a little nuisance. A HUGE nuisance. You destroyed our nice time together in the lab. Our camaraderie. Our joy when a compound works and gives expected results. Everything is gone now. I can't be friends with my blackmailer.

(He looks at her with sadness. She's touched but wouldn't admit it.)

MIA. We don't need to be friends. We can just... work together.

10.

*(**ADAM** and **KARA** in a coffee shop.)*

ADAM. She's insane, I'm telling you. I wish I knew that from the beginning, I would have never accepted her in my program!

KARA. Shhhh. People can hear us. She's not crazy, she's sort of a genius. She's been like that since she was little, she'd never socialize much, she didn't have any friends, just books, books, books and notebooks. She'd take notes about everything. The crumbles of bread on the table, the cracks on the floor, in the wall...

ADAM. She needs to see a specialist, the girl has parasites in the... *(pointing at his head)* "attic".

KARA. Right, the solution for everything: a shrink. How American you've become. Treating the symptoms, not the causes... Anything else you wanted to tell me?

ADAM. She stopped our experiment on reproductive cheaters! That experiment helped us understand the ways ants and other social insects communicate. Through pheromone signaling. It's a huge discovery! It's not just about ants, their behavioral patterns help us make huge progress in the study of aging. It's for people too. The temptation to cheat exists in any society, from insects to humans, although the methods of "reproductive policing" may be different. Social harmony is dependent on strict systems to prevent and punish cheating individuals. But why am I telling you all this...

KARA. To justify cheating on your wife maybe?

ADAM. You didn't get a word from what I said.

KARA. I didn't get the details, but I got the main points. Mia thinks you're framing those poor ants for this "huge discovery". But I can actually understand that some people, pardon, ants must be sacrificed for... progress. Like the Tarot card of The Hanged Man, a sacrifice restores balance. A person is like a little ant, she needs all the others to survive, she must sacrifice her own interest for the greater good, for the good of all society.

ADAM. Yeah, something like that.

KARA. You see… Mia is probably still a virgin. Those hormones mess her up.

ADAM. I don't know what to do with her. I'm OK with giving money to you, I'm OK with that, it's for our baby. But that crazy little Virgin Mary can spoil everything.

KARA. Don't call her that.

ADAM. You know what. Enough about Mia. How do YOU feel? How do you spend your days?

KARA. Doing nothing. Well. Except for Tarot readings, a little I-Ching maybe…

ADAM. Are you good at that kinda stuff?

KARA. I've become an expert.

ADAM. Shall I send you some paying customers?

KARA. Like who? - your wife's girlfriends?

ADAM. People make money from that. Beth paid 200 dollars to a Gypsy lady who "cleansed our house of bad energies"…

KARA. *(ironically)* And I "cleansed your aura" weekly for free.

(They laugh. A tensed laugh.)

ADAM. We need a relief from all this bad energy and tension. I have an hour at my disposal. Let's go to the motel.

KARA. No.

ADAM. C'mon, you need a little fun too.

KARA. I told you it's over, Adam.

ADAM. But… we have something now. Together.

KARA. There's no "together". It has never been.

ADAM. You're irritable. It's normal in the first trimester of pregnancy.

KARA. Fuck "normal". Nothing is normal. I don't want this baby!

ADAM. You must look at the facts, Kara: you're almost 40. It might be… your only chance to have a child.

KARA. Why? You think you're the only man who'd sleep with me?

ADAM. No, it's just… you're not getting any younger.

KARA. *(standing up)* Thanks. For the coffee.

ADAM. *(stopping her)* Wait. Sorry. I didn't mean / to…

KARA. Listen, Adam. I gave you five years of my life. You owe me this: give Mia a real job. Take care of her.

ADAM. Kara, / I…

KARA. I'm gonna go now. I have a meeting in 15 minutes. With my daily nausea.

(She leaves. He stares at her leaving.)

11.

*(**MIA** is in the backyard of their house, checking on the nest of ants.)*

MIA. *(to the audience)* Marx and Engels, you're right. With that Communist Manifesto. "Class antagonisms...The exploitation of one part of society by the other"... I used to hate that quote, to think it's just propaganda. Now I understand it better. I can see it applied everywhere. But in the ants' world I can make a difference, I can. The nest we created in the lab is a capitalist nest. It has exploitation, injustice, struggle... This one here is a communist nest, everybody is equal. We don't need males here, not even for reproduction. My ants can decide when they want to emanate the fertility scent, to begin procreating, and no one interferes with that. My ants are not attacking each other. They live like sisters. Full, rich and safe lives. Communism meets Amazonia!

12.

(**MIA** *and* **KARA** *are in their house's courtyard.*)

KARA. I don't like to look at the ants, Mia, I'm sorry, I don't like them.

MIA. You don't like ants' infestation, the ants that nest in homes and destroy furniture, but... This nest we have here is a peaceful one. They don't bother you if you don't bother them. They only eat your garbage. Look, they work together beautifully. They help and feed each other. They take care of the eggs, see, there.

KARA. *(looking at the nest)* Those are the eggs? They're like little salt spots.

MIA. Exactly.

KARA. OK, let's go inside, I'm cold.

MIA. We need to talk about Pupa.

KARA. What's to talk about? It grows inside me. It makes me vomit. It makes me irritable.

MIA. I answered the phone when you were in the bathroom. It was a lady confirming your appointment. With the abortion clinic.

KARA. Yes, I decided to go. And not tell anyone about it. It's my body, my decision.

(Silence.)

MIA. But you promised me...

KARA. I said I'd wait a few days, until you got a job. You didn't get any job.

MIA. But I got money for us. Adam is paying child support. Well, baby-in-the-belly support.

KARA. That's not what I wanted. I told you to leave him out of this. You spoiled everything.

MIA. But we need the money.

KARA. I don't want his money. Ew, I got an ant on my leg. (*She shakes her leg.*)

MIA. Don't kill her!

KARA. I'm going inside. I had enough of this... ants-zoo. In my own backyard. You study ants at the lab, why did you have to do this here?

MIA. I brought a queen and I let her create the colony from scratch. It was magnificent to see it growing. Then I removed the queen / and -

KARA. Great. Growing a colony of ants in my backyard. I guess I should be grateful you didn't bring them in the house. In the kitchen. To eat at the same table with us.

(**KARA** *walks away.*)

MIA. Be careful not to step on them!

(**KARA** *stops and acts like she's ready to step on the ants.*)

KARA. What if I step on them and kill a few, who's gonna care? They just multiply and multiply, that's their karma, working and multiplying, working and/ multiplying -

MIA. Please, don't. It's their nest. Their home. You wouldn't like to have your house destroyed, would you?

KARA. Actually, I would. Then nothing would keep me here ... I'd move to New York and open a small fortune-telling business. Tarot and I-Ching readings, astrology, numerology, anything. Tell people that nothing is fixed, you can start all over again if you want...

I'd finally benefit from all those "exciting" evenings filled with horoscopes and DO-IT-YOURSELF TAROT. I'll do it for others. I can now open myself to a question and the Universe answers me. I feel all this energy growing inside me.

MIA. It's the baby.

KARA. No, it's not the baby.

MIA. It's Pupa, she's the new energy. It's the chemical signal of you being pregnant.

KARA. No, it's not in my belly. It's somewhere else, in my brain, and down here, in my heart. It's even in my legs, asking me to go, go, go, far away...

(She walks towards the house without stepping on the ants' rest.)

MIA. But. We have this beautiful house. You know how many people back home would die to have a house like this: four rooms, a backyard, a deck? Don't you remember us crammed in two rooms, mom and dad sleeping on a couch in the living room and the two of us in the bedroom? You forgot all that.

KARA. I don't need a big house. I could live in a small one-bedroom apartment in New York and use the living room for readings. Why struggle to be like everyone else here: work, work, work, house, car, husband, kids? I'm sooo tired of pushing, pushing, towards... what?... the American dream? I'd rather have my own little nightmare.

MIA. You can't just... pack and go. There are ... things... responsibilities... people who are relying on you: mom, pupa, me...

KARA. Right, YOU are actually my baby. Do me a big, big favor: grow up!

(She heads towards the house. **MIA** *is speechless.)*

13.

*(MIA writes a huge "U" on the front wall of their house.
She stops, turn towards the audience and addresses it.)*

MIA. There are extraordinary circumstances when creating
a synthetic compound to attract attention is acceptable.
When your act is actually a form of nurturing. When
the goal excuses the means.

What we must do now, as the first step of transforming
a worker into a queen, is to make the eggs impossible
to be recognized as "second-class". I was wrong to focus
on the workers, we must see what can be done for the
eggs now.

For our little Pupa...

*(The Biochemistry Lab. ADAM is immersed in a
microscope observation. MIA is recording.)*

ADAM. Your synthetic hydrocarbon seems to work well on
the eggs. They are not being destroyed by the other
ants, so they must be seen as the queen's eggs.

MIA. Yes, it's working. I'm beginning to be quite fluent in
this hydrocarbon sign language. Soon I could write a
whole dictionary.

ADAM. What dictionary: food, war, reproduction, egg, larva,
pupa, worker, soldier, queen... anything else you can
think of?

MIA. Worker-queen.

ADAM. That would be impossible. The ants will be perceived
as either workers or queens. There are no hyphenated
words in the ants' world.

MIA. I want to make them realize that it's OK to be both.

ADAM. That's a bit too much to ask from the poor
brainless ants. I thought we're working on making a
few workers queens and I give you that, I've grown to
find this experiment quite fascinating, it can help us
understand better the aging process too, we can see
how long the worker turned queen lives compared to

the worker that remains a worker. The NYU researchers are already making a lot of progress in a study about epigenetics' influence on behavior and aging.

MIA. I'm not particularly interested in the studies of aging.

ADAM. You should be. It's a field that's new and growing, I mean really growing.

What's the matter? We are getting closer to your dream, the workers we "framed" will soon be recognized as queens. Isn't that what you wanted?

MIA. I want more now.

ADAM. You can have them start new colonies.

MIA. I want workers to be treated like queens.

ADAM. That's possible in a colony without a queen, you know that. Everybody there is equal and they can reproduce as they please. A true democratic society compared to the totalitarian one with a queen. You can draw a parallel that involves social psychology and even political studies.

MIA. *(compulsively)* I want to make a difference in the ants' life! I don't want just to study them, I want to help them!

ADAM. Mia, your behavior worries me. You should see somebody.

MIA. Like what, a man? Have sex with somebody? With you, maybe?

ADAM. I'm not gonna say an extra word about that. I'm not sexually harassing you, OK? I'm worried as a teacher for his favorite student.

We made some very interesting new explorations thanks to you, we can write together an article summing up our new study about the worker turned queen. We can publish it in Current Biology. Your career can progress very well, Mia, you're closer than ever to that teaching position. I could even get you the Dean's Fellowship for outstanding research. Don't screw everything up. Please.

MIA. <u>You</u> screwed everything up. Kara has an appointment for an abortion on Thursday morning at 11 am. We must go there before it happens. Stop her literally.

ADAM. I don't know if it's wise for me to go there. It would make it clear to everybody that it's my baby... Kara doesn't want that. It won't help.

MIA. I've already taken a few important steps. I created a "pregnancy" signal for her. Similar to the chemical signal of the reproductive ants, but you know, in the humans' language.

ADAM. What did you do?

MIA. I wrote on the front wall of our house, with a non-washable marker, in big capital letters: UNEMPLOYED PREGNANT WOMAN. DON'T LET HER HAVE AN ABORTION!

ADAM. That's NOT gonna help.

MIA. I also wrote it on her car. There's no way to hide it now, people will know about it. The society will impose its self-regulating rules. Any neighbor or person at the supermarket will address that somehow.

ADAM. You lost your freakin' mind.

MIA. Do you want your Pupa to be born or not?

ADAM. Pupa?

MIA. Your baby.

ADAM. We are not ants, Mia. Wake up! There are similarities between the ant society and the human one, but there are also HUGE differences. We have a consciousness, a brain. We make decisions for ourselves.

MIA. The ants make decisions too. Like five minutes ago you were drawing parallels between the two societies.

ADAM. Regarding the process of aging and the factors that influence it.

MIA. Like behavior and reproductive policies. It's exactly what I'm talking about.

ADAM. OK. I'm calling Kara, I have to talk with her directly.

MIA. No! She doesn't want to hear from you. You must come to our house on Thursday morning. People won't think anything bad, you'll come to take me to the Lab or check on my ants nest, something like that.

ADAM. I'm not sure this / is a good -

MIA. We must stop her, Adam.

ADAM. *(beat)* You'll say I'm there for a research matter, yes? You won't frame me.

MIA. I swear on my never getting the Nobel Prize.

ADAM. *(inappropriately amused)* OK, I'll be at your house at 9 am.

MIA. Thank you.

ADAM. I've never been to your house, you know.

MIA. She never invited you?

ADAM. Never.

MIA. Well, I invite you.

(a short awkward moment)

ADAM. Let's see what those little queens are doing.

(They go back to the microscope.)

14.

(MIA's and KARA's house. MIA opens the door for ADAM. They enter the living room together.)

ADAM. What you did on the wall... Crazy. You shouldn't have done that. Where is Kara?

MIA. She's not up yet. Yesterday when I got home at 8.30, she was already sleeping. I don't know what to do. Wake her up? This is not like her.

ADAM. Let her sleep.

MIA. She's always up at 7, even on weekends she can't sleep more than 8. And now is 9.15!

ADAM. It must be the pregnancy. Your biorhythm changes. *(looking around)* You guys have a nice house. Well-decorated...

MIA. It's big. You should see the backyard, I LOVE the backyard, we kinda have our own forest.

ADAM. Kara must have worked hard for all / this...

MIA. Do you want a coffee or something?

ADAM. Coffee sounds good.

(MIA gestures towards the table: two cups with coffee are waiting for them.)

MIA. I've already made the coffee. Couldn't focus on anything else.

(Shared silence. They are both immersed in their thoughts but they somehow seem connected to each other. Like they're working together on the "We don't need to be embarrassed by this weird and unexpected intimacy" experiment.)

ADAM. *(sips from his coffee)* It's a good sign if she misses the appointment. It means that deep down her conscience she doesn't want to do it.

MIA. *(sips from her coffee)* I'm worried. Something is not right.

ADAM. I don't think it's good for her to find me here.

MIA. Please, wait half an hour. To be sure she doesn't get to the appointment.

(They sip their coffees. Silence.)

ADAM. Guess what. One of your worker ants separated from the nest.

MIA. *(excited)* Really?!

ADAM. She couldn't move too far but she behaves like a queen, she seems to want to start a new colony, to begin laying eggs. I'm not sure yet, but I think she's growing wings too.

MIA. YES! Can't wait to see her! Did you go to the lab first thing in the morning?

ADAM. I slept there. On the couch in my office.

MIA. Why didn't you go home? You wanted to be the first one who sees the queen-worker, that's not fair!

ADAM. I didn't plan that. I just… it was too late to drive for an hour, it didn't make much sense.

MIA. But you never sleep in the lab.

ADAM. I was feeling tired.

MIA. You wanted to be the first. Admit it.

ADAM. You'll be the first one to see her growing wings, mating, laying eggs. I promise.

MIA. That wasn't fair…

ADAM. It wasn't premeditated.

(KARA appears. She has huge black circles around her eyes, she looks sick.)

KARA. What is he doing here?

ADAM. *(standing up)* Good morning, Kara. I just came to take Mia to the lab. Our experiment gave an unexpected positive result.

MIA. You look like shit, are you feeling OK?

KARA. I had an awful dream. I was giving birth to a fucking ant and it was growing and growing and growing and I had to breast feed her but I couldn't because she was so ugly and disgusting. And she kept growing until she

almost crushed me under her weight. Then she grew
wings and tried to fly but the ceiling would stop her so
she'd come back to me, to crush me again and again.
But she wasn't really crushing me, she was writing
on me: "Unemployed Pregnant Woman"... Horrible
dream. You and your ants... leave me alone. Go to
your lab.

MIA. You don't look good. We should take you to the
hospital. This doesn't look like a normal nausea.

KARA. Like you know what's a normal nausea.

ADAM. She's right. You don't look well.

(**KARA** *pours herself coffee.* **MIA** *tries to help.*)

KARA. I can do it.

MIA. We just... we wanted to make sure you're OK. You've
never slept until 9. There are probably things changing
in your body because your condition but still, you
must / be careful -

KARA. There's no "condition" anymore.

MIA. What do you mean?

KARA. I got rid of that little ant in my belly.

MIA. That's not possible. Your appointment was / for today.

KARA. You think you're smart. I'm smarter. I changed the
appointment. I went yesterday afternoon. It's done.

ADAM. You had an abortion?

MIA. No!

KARA. Yes. (*to* **ADAM**) There's no such thing as "our" baby
anymore, there's nothing that we have "together".
Nothing. I'm free.

ADAM. You shouldn't have done this.

KARA. It's my body. My mistake. My decision. I'm not an
ant in your lab, to pour fertility chemicals on me and
see how I give birth and how other ants attack me. I
understand everything about your "experiment", I'm
not dumb.

MIA. We stopped that study. We are now changing worker ants into queens so they can reproduce / freely -

KARA. Reproduce, reproduce! Give me a break with your reproduction. Why should they, why should we reproduce? To bring more ants into this world, to ride the Wheel of Fortune, up and down, up and down, down and down, breakfast, car, work, work, lunch break, work, dinner, TV, ants, ants, ants…

(She faints.)

MIA. Kara! Let's take her to the hospital!

ADAM. Help me put her on the bed.

*(He checks her pulse and her temperature. **KARA** moans.)*

She's gonna be OK. She's exhausted. Emotionally more than physically. She just needs to relax. In a supportive environment.

MIA. I'll stay home with her.

ADAM. I should have called her yesterday…

MIA. I should have checked with the clinic again…

ADAM. Well. What's done is done.

MIA. We could have stopped it.

ADAM. Could. Should. It doesn't matter anymore. Maybe this is the best for her.

15.

*(**MIA** paints the front wall of the house white, addressing the audience.)*

MIA. My worker-ant is growing wings! I should be sooo happy, but… (Kara)

Let's see how she responds to the wings' growing. Is she gonna fly to mate with a male? Or choose to do it by herself…What if she chooses not to mate and not to do it by herself? That's impossible. Then she's not a queen, is she?

(change of tone – she stops painting)

Kara's abortion is my fault. I changed the environment, I triggered a new set of consequences. I wish I could paint this past week white and write new deeds on it.

How can I still give Kara wings? Is money wings? Is love wings? Hope? Fun? Relaxation? A plane ticket to Cancun? To Paris? To fucking Jamaica?

What gives wings to humans?

16.

*(**ADAM** and **MIA** in the Lab, observing the ants.)*

ADAM. It should happen AFTER the mating ritual.

MIA. I can't believe she got rid of her wings.

ADAM. It's genetic, I told you.

MIA. But she could reproduce, make her eggs look like the queen's eggs, give them a chance to a different life!

ADAM. She knows she's not really a queen, even if we made the other ants take her for one.

MIA. I thought she'd start a new colony.

ADAM. She doesn't have what it takes. The genetic drive.

MIA. No, it can't be that. In a nourishing environment, if she's treated like a queen since she's an egg, she'll start to behave like a queen. We need to change the focus: the eggs. It's about the eggs! We give them "princess" chemical scent, they'll develop into queens! Real queens, believing they are meant to be queens.

ADAM. The old nature versus nurture debate. Your bet is on nurture. Mine is on nature.

MIA. So… are we doing it? Shall I prepare the compound for the eggs?

ADAM. Are you taking the bet?

MIA. Yes. If you nurture them appropriately, they will become queens while other eggs with the same genetic attributes will just be workers or soldiers.

ADAM. And what do I get if I'm right?

MIA. Nothing. Or. What? A sandwich? A coffee? A book? *(joking)* A kick in the ass? A kiss? But you're not right, you'll see.

ADAM. A kiss. Without a sexual harassment complaint attached to it.

(A little awkward moment.)

MIA. I'm gonna prepare the hydrocarbon.

ADAM. It's 9 pm, leave it for tomorrow.

MIA. No, I must do it today so we can apply it tomorrow.

ADAM. I can drive you home if we leave now. How's your sister doing?

MIA. She doesn't talk much. She's immersed in Tarot readings, I-Ching, Mandala, Feng Shui, you name it... She walks around home "cleansing energies". But I'm glad she's into something.

ADAM. She should see somebody. A therapist I mean.

MIA. That's a good "joke", Adam. Like we have money for a therapist when a foreclosure is looming over our heads...

ADAM. Listen. I meant to tell you this earlier. I kept waiting for the right moment. Take a seat.

MIA. What? You're not firing me, are you?

ADAM. *(beat)* You got the Dean's Fellowship.

MIA. What?!

ADAM. Yeah. I recommended you and you got it. 35,000 dollars, baby.

MIA. You're not kidding, are you?

ADAM. I told the Dean: help my best researcher focus on her work! And she agreed.

MIA. Adam, this is... I mean this is like really...Oh, my God!... So I'll get all that money?! I've never had that kind of money in my life.

ADAM. You'll get it in two installments. 20,000 upfront, 15,000 at the end of the semester.

MIA. I can focus on research!!! *(beat)* We can pay the bills... and the mortgage... we can keep the house! (*She starts jumping like a child.*)

ADAM. See, you gotta go home and tell Kara.

(*Pause.* **MIA** *is speechlessly happy.*)

MIA. Adam... You really... I mean... you've just washed away all your sins, Adam.

ADAM. You deserve this fellowship, Mia. You are my best
    researcher.

17.

(MIA *enters the living room.* KARA *is at the table, doing a Tarot reading for herself.*)

MIA. What are the cards telling you?

KARA. *(showing her a card)* The Star. It means I should trust my intuition. I should do whatever I feel like doing. I'm attuned to divine wisdom.

MIA. *(half-joking)* You should do one of those readings for me too.

KARA. You don't believe in Tarot.

MIA. I'm curious.

KARA. You really want a reading? Are you sure?

MIA. Yes.

KARA. Come over here.

MIA. *(sitting at the table)* OK. Shoot.

KARA. Shoot?!

MIA. It means "go on".

KARA. I know what it means. But you never used it before.

MIA. Do I have to think of anything in particular?

KARA. Yes, focus on an issue that you want illuminated by this reading.

MIA. "Illuminated"?

KARA. Get answers or insights.

MIA. All right. I'm thinking of something.

KARA. *(arranges the cards on the table)* OK. Pick a card.

(MIA *picks a card and shows it to* KARA.)

KARA. Very interesting. Three of coins. You're able to do something out of nothing. This is the so-called Genius card.

MIA. I like this game.

KARA. Pick another one.

MIA. No, no, I don't want this Genius card spoiled with a... Broken Heart or Death or something.

KARA. C'mon, we need three cards.

MIA. OK. *(She picks one and shows it to **KARA**.)* This one doesn't look good.

KARA. It's the Hermit in the Challenges position. The Hermit is old but at heart he's actually a child, never ceasing to wonder, to question and explore the universe.

MIA. What does that mean?

KARA. You spend too much time alone. You're studying life in all its forms.

MIA. Nothing new.

KARA. Your challenge is to try to connect with people. To find a soul-mate.

MIA. OK...

KARA. Pick another one.

MIA. The last one. *(She picks one and shows it to **KARA**.)*

KARA. Ten of coins. That's a good one. It means you are moving among the Privileged. It means wealth, money...

MIA. You know what... there's some truth in this game.

KARA. Maybe they'll give you a teaching position.

MIA. *(standing up)* OK. Don't move. Don't faint. Tah-dah-daaaam! I got the Dean's Fellowship!

KARA. How much?

MIA. 35,000! 20,000 next week, the rest in June!

KARA. Oh, my God, Mia!

MIA. Yes, yes, yes!

*(She throws some Tarot cards up in the air. **KARA** joins her.)*

KARA. Yes!

MIA. *(dancing)* Money, money, money!

(They both dance, happy, singing the Abba refrain.)

KARA/MIA. Money, money, money! Money, money, money - must be funny… in the rich man's world…!

KARA. This is good. It's great!

MIA. We can keep the house. We can pay the bills. We are saved.

KARA. You can stay in the house. I don't have to worry about you anymore.

MIA. What are you talking about? It's WE.

KARA. I can go to New York now.

(Pause.)

MIA. You can't be serious.

KARA. I still have Adam's money: 4000 dollars. I was thinking to give it back, but… He knows what's what. No hard feelings. Just a sense of closure. And justice.

MIA. Adam is not a bad guy. He understands. *(beat)* He got me the grant.

KARA. I was his whore, I deserve the money.

MIA. Kara, nobody associates the word "whore" with you.

KARA. Except everybody in the neighborhood and the people at the supermarket. They look at me / like -

MIA. I'll tell everyone it was a… joke, a prank. You lost at poker!

KARA. *(ironically)* Yeah, I got poked…

MIA. I painted the front wall, you can't see those letters anymore.

KARA. You didn't paint white my brain too.

MIA. C'mon, Kara… I'm sorry, I really am. We'll make things right. We have money now. *(singing)* Money, money, money…

KARA. *(without singing)* Always sunny, in the rich man's world… I can rent a one-bedroom in Queens. I checked. It's 1100 a month.

MIA. When do you wanna leave?

KARA. On Monday. The best day for a fresh start.

18.

*(**MIA** is the backyard of the house, studying the ants'
nest. She addresses the audience.)*

MIA. Most ants establish new colonies through swarming.
However, the percentage of queens that successfully
begin new colonies is very, very small... An inseminated
queen rids herself of her wings and attempts to start a
new nest in a cavity, under a stone or a piece of bark,
or by excavating a hole in the ground ... For a while,
she's all alone there, in her little retreat... She waits,
she takes her chances... Mating was just the starting
point, the zero moment of her new life, of a whole
colony's life... *(change of tone)* Mating.... I must explore
this mating thing further... there are things I don't
fully comprehend because... Virginity Complex? I
need to do more research on this.

19.

(MIA enters the Lab. ADAM looks slightly disheveled.)

MIA. You slept in your office again…

ADAM. It's just until… I find a nice little place for myself. A small house, an apartment… *(beat)*
Beth and I… are taking a break.

MIA. What happened?

(ADAM has an outburst, but there is something truthful about it:)

ADAM. Nothing happened. I just realized that actually nothing happens between us, absolutely nothing. She's a wonderful person, kind, balanced, but there's nothing between us. No flux of feelings. No communication. Nothing. Just silence interrupted by sentences like "Do you like the new antique vase that I bought for the salon? – Yes, honey. You have exquisite taste, as always." "Did you order French shampoo for the dogs? Yes, honey." "Did you give a good tip to the gardener? Yes, of course, honey."

MIA. What about your kids?

ADAM. They are big now, in college, working. The house is empty without them. And I can see Elisabeth better. I can see that all we have in common are the kids.

MIA. That's good enough.

ADAM. No, that's not good enough. *(beat)*
Enough personal drama. Back to work. Let's inspect the ants' nest.

(MIA does so too.)

You can see that the born-queen's eggs are much bigger than the worker's eggs. Your compound will help them not to be recognized and destroyed for a while but not forever.

MIA. For 6-8 weeks, until they become adults. Winged adults.

ADAM. OK, let's say that we can apply this compound for 6-8 weeks.

MIA. I've already done it for two weeks, there's one month left.

ADAM. You still need to nurture them for at least one year to have them grow as big as the real queens.

MIA. I will. I will apply the compound regularly. I can take some of them home, so I apply the hydrocarbon both in the morning and in the evening every day.

ADAM. Kara will kill you if you bring more ants at home.

MIA. Kara is gone, she moved to New York.

ADAM. She did?

MIA. She's resetting her life. A fresh start. As a fortune-teller.

ADAM. Well. If that makes her happy...

MIA. She had to go. To cut the "umbilical" cord between me and her. And the weird post-abortion post-affair post-cord between you and her.

ADAM. Let's make things clear once forever. I and Kara enjoyed each other's company, in those particular, uncommitted terms. I am sorry if I hurt her in any way, it wasn't my intention. I thought the circumstances were clear for both of us.

MIA. Adultery is the quintessence of unclear, Adam. Anyway. A kick in the ass is a step forward. She needed badly some change in her life, a "hope compound". She's growing wings now.

ADAM. Tell her... I wish her... good luck and silver wings.

MIA. Very poetic.

(Pause.)

ADAM. Do you hate me too?

MIA. I hated you for about... 2 hours and three vodka tonics, at a stupid party in the campus.

ADAM. Good to know. You go to parties in the campus?

MIA. Just once. After Kara told me about the two of you.

ADAM. *(beat)* And who's taking care of you now if Kara's gone?

MIA. Do I seem to need a babysitter?

ADAM. Not a babysitter, just a "daily-care" compound.

MIA. I can take care of myself, thanks, Adam. Actually I enjoy being alone in the whole house. Nobody is disturbing my research.

ADAM. You'll become a hermit.

MIA. Right, what a cliché for a scientist.

(**ADAM** *considers whether he should continue the personal conversation.*)

ADAM. Don't do that, Mia. You're an attractive woman, it's a shame to close yourself up to life. Life in all its forms and shapes and emotions and desires...

MIA. I've been thinking about that actually. I have to do it before I turn 30.

ADAM. You'll start dating?

MIA. I created an application form. All healthy males aged between 20 and 50 can apply.

ADAM. *(joking)* I still qualify. What's this form about?

MIA. *(showing him a form.)* They can apply to mate with me. It's the Losing-My-Virginity event. I scheduled it for next Sunday between 5 and 8 pm, when I'm at the peak of my monthly fertility curve.

ADAM. Between 5 and 8?

MIA. If things go well, I might extend it to the whole night. I mention that at the end of the application form. Do you want one?

ADAM. This is a bit... abrupt, Mia. Are you sure this is the way you want to have your first sexual experience? It should be more... romantic, it should be about love.

MIA. It's just about mating. Love is not something I'm prepared to research right now. Love might actually be out of my league in terms of research. It's a too complex and irrational chemical equation. I am not ready to study it.

ADAM. *(perplexed)* But Mia…

MIA. But, but, but! There's no but, just butt. Your words.

ADAM. To lose your virginity with some immature horny student who doesn't / know what -

MIA. I'll be very careful with the selection process.

ADAM. Where did you advertise… THIS?

MIA. On the student e-lists, posters in the campus. I want someone from the academic world, he must have certain genetic attributes.

ADAM. Aha, back to nature! Genetic attributes.

MIA. I can't take the risk that I'm taking with the ants' eggs with my own possible baby. I want to apply a nature and nurture mix in this case.

ADAM. The bottom line is: you arrived at my conclusion. Genes are important. I won the bet.

MIA. OK, maybe, yeah, I owe you a kiss.

ADAM. Of course genetic characteristics are crucial, you can't…

(MIA kisses him on the cheek timidly.)

MIA. There. I paid my debt.

ADAM. OK…

MIA. Gotta go now. To put some applications at the Health Center.

ADAM. That's ridiculous. You can't / just…

MIA. Why not? I can leave a few at the reception… (*She's about to leave.*)

ADAM. Wait. Can I have one of those application forms?

20.

KARA. Dear Mia,

I am enjoying New York VERY much. There are so many people here and you don't need a car, you just take the subway or walk, and you are among people! I always liked human beings, these unpredictable creatures with emotions, feelings, problems, passions, marriages, divorces... This is what makes life exciting, Mia. For me at least. You like to study ants, I like to study people, to help them, give them someone who listens to their stories, someone who can talk with them about themselves, everyone wants that in the depth of his/her heart... I don't know how much money I can make with these Tarot and I-Ching readings, but I know that people love to hear about their destiny, their present, their future, even their past. I guess it makes them feel... alive. I have many Latino and Black clients. And it's full of immigrants from everywhere! Nobody cares about your accent. Everybody has an accent. Finally a neighborhood that's not all white and stiff as ours over there, where nobody would visit us or say hello on the street. Except for that crazy day when you wrote that thing about me on the wall. That day, lots of people came to our door to look down at me and preach and make me feel like trash... I'm happy I had the abortion, Mia. I know you can't understand this, with your ants and obsession, sorry, research on reproductive patterns. But it freed myself, Mia. It gave me wings and I know wings matter to you almost as much as reproduction. So be happy, sister, and let those ants rest at least on weekend! Go out, enjoy life, people, find someone to love you, grow wings, you know how to do it, you're the specialist. Lots of love, your sister, Kara.

PS: Thanks for the 2000 dollars. They've been very very helpful...

PPS: I'm dating! I met this guy, Pedro. What a man...

21.

(The Losing-My-Virginity Sunday.)

*(**MIA** paces the living room back and forth.)*

(She's made some effort to wear a nice dress and make up. She looks very pretty.)

MIA. I'm not nervous. I'm not nervous. I'm not nervous. It's nothing special. Just mating. An exchange of fluids.

*(The bell rings. **MIA** is paralyzed. The bell rings again. And again.)*

MIA. Oh, God!

(She goes off-stage to open the door.)

*(She comes back with **ADAM**.)*

(He holds a bouquet of flowers and seems nervous too.)

ADAM. I've never seen you wearing a dress. You look veeery pretty.

MIA. Thanks.

ADAM. *(handing the flowers)* For you.

MIA. Thanks.

(Awkward silence.)

ADAM. Can I take a seat?

MIA. Sure. Please.

*(**ADAM** sits on the couch. Awkward silence.)*

ADAM. Come. Sit next to me.

MIA. Not yet. I'm OK with standing. For now.

ADAM. Don't worry. You won't lose your virginity on this couch. We will use a bed. I hope.

MIA. Yes, a bed would be more appropriate.

(Awkward silence.)

ADAM. *(attempting to joke)* I'm happy I got selected.

MIA. Well…

(Awkward silence.)

ADAM. Was it difficult – the selection process?

MIA. There were serious arguments against you. You're my sister's ex-lover.

ADAM. May I emphasize the EX?

MIA. I'm not sure if Kara... would like this.

ADAM. I'm sure what matters for her more is for you to be in safe hands. *(pause)* So ... How many people applied?

MIA. *(beat)* I guess men don't find me pretty enough to mate with me. No one else applied.

ADAM. That's not true, you're very pretty. When you want to be. When you don't shut up your estrogen signals.

MIA. I didn't emit the right fertility signal, that's why nobody applied?

ADAM. You mentioned "no condom" in the application form. Young men today don't want to take the risk of having a child. Or get an STD. / Or -

MIA. Not even the ugliest nerd.

ADAM. I hope I'm not worse than the ugliest nerd.

MIA. You're not worse, it's just...

ADAM. The professor-student thing?

MIA. It's gonna be weird to work together after this.

ADAM. Why? We have covered all the possible discussions on reproductive patterns.

MIA. In theory, yes.

ADAM. Take it like an experiment. That's how you advertised it.

MIA. Of course. Yes. It is an experiment. And I mentioned STD-free in the application form!

(Awkward silence.)

ADAM. How are our ants doing?

MIA. It's going very well. The size of the worker's larva is growing closer to the one of the queen's.

ADAM. Good. Do you apply the compound twice a day?

MIA. Three times, just to make sure that nothing unexpected happens. But only one time for the eggs in the lab, so we can see the difference when we apply different degrees of nurturing.

ADAM. Have you finished the first draft of the article?

MIA. Not yet. But I'm taking notes daily.

ADAM. We'll also have to work on a lecture version, to present at the LAMA conference in May…

MIA. We still have 8 months for that. I'm / practicing…

ADAM. You gotta finish the essay. You'll be revising it, but it's very important to write down the first thoughts on an experiment, freshness and spontaneity give the most profound insights.

MIA. I know.

(Silence.)

ADAM. I should have brought a little bottle of red wine. Or whisky, or champagne.

MIA. I have red wine. Bordeaux. Is that OK?

ADAM. Perfect.

MIA. I'm not sure what's the effect of red wine on the process. Of mating. It might affect it negatively.

ADAM. It generally affects it positively.

MIA. All right then.

(She brings a bottle of red wine and two champagne glasses.)

ADAM. These are champagne glasses.

MIA. I have champagne too. I wasn't sure what would be the most appropriate… for the process.

ADAM. Red wine is fine.

(He pours red wine in the champagne glasses.)

MIA. Yes

(He hands her a glass.)

Cheers!

ADAM. Cheers!

(Silence.)

MIA. For the experiment!

ADAM. Which one are we talking about?

MIA. Because it's you and not another applicant, we are toasting first for THE BIG experiment, the Nobel Prize winning experiment, and then we get into my little personal one.

ADAM. Cheers, for the Nobel Prize!

MIA. For the Nobel Prize!

ADAM. And for Mia's Virginity Prize!

MIA. You're making fun of me.

ADAM. No, honey.

MIA. Don't call me "honey" like in your breaking-the-silence daily ritual with your wife.

ADAM. Ex-wife.

MIA. She's still legally your wife.

(They drink.)

ADAM. Beth asked for a divorce. It's the right thing to do.

*(**MIA** downs the glass and fills it again herself.)*

MIA. I keep thinking of her. We nicknamed her The Queen, me and Kara...

ADAM. Your application form didn't mention "never married and virgin"...

(He fills the glasses. They drink.)

MIA. I'm sorry. That was too... emotional. I'm trying to avoid that. *(she drinks)*
So what would be the first step for... you know, the process of mating.

ADAM. Please, call it sex. Or making love.

(He takes her hand.)

This is the first step.

MIA. I read about a few stages called: the first base, the second, the third and the home run.

ADAM. We'll go through all the stages. Patience, my dear.

(They drink. He caresses her face. He kisses her tenderly.)

ADAM. How was that?

MIA. Unexpectedly… sweet.

ADAM. Shall I… apply the compound again?

MIA. Sure. Definitely. Again. *(giggles)* And again. Wow. It must be the red wine, I'm talking too much.

(He kisses her again. And again.)

ADAM. Good?

MIA. Not bad.

(He kisses her again tenderly. She kisses him back, aggressively.)

ADAM. Little lioness! Bit me…

MIA. I didn't bite you.

(They kiss again, passionately.)

(They stop, they're surprised – it's too good!)

ADAM. Are we still talking 5-8 pm or I can start thinking "the whole night"?

MIA. "Whole night" sounds surprisingly plausible.

(They drink.)

ADAM. What about "whole life", how does that sound?

(She spills red wine on her blouse. They look at each other and laugh.)

ADAM. Is that a yes?

MIA. I dunno … I think… we need to wait… to be more advanced in the process.

ADAM. It's a "maybe".

MIA. Maybe…

ADAM. Are you gonna put some cold water on those stains?

MIA. I should?

ADAM. No. Stains are sexy. Bio-chemically speaking.

MIA. Can we start mating now?

(They kiss. Lights fade.)

(A projection of a short film with ants and a cheerful soundtrack. A queen-ant is a must in the film.)

(Spotlight on **KARA** *dressing up for a date, looking in a mirror. She looks good, she's happy with herself, she heads out.)*

(The ants film is now cross-cut or overlapped with a sort of calendar of Tarot cards, sliding away one by one.)

(Back to the film with ants.)

22.

*(A few months later. **MIA**, visibly pregnant, dressed for the conference, addresses the audience.)*

MIA. Thank you, from all my heart – and my belly

(Recorded laughter and applause.)

– for the opportunity to be in front of you today, to present the results of our experiment THE WORKER-QUEEN. I and Professor Adam Kohn, my PhD thesis advisor and my husband,

(recorded applauses)

are very pleased to have succeeded to demonstrate that social roles in ants colonies can be modified chemically not only genetically.

Our experiment proves that NURTURING worker-ants and their eggs with the right chemical compound can not only change the way in which the worker-ants are perceived by the other ants, but also the way in which they perceive themselves. Not only their reproductive behavior has changed from sterile workers to horny queens,

(recorded laughter)

but their eggs received royal treatment and subsequently their larvae and pupae were perceived as royal. After six months of sustained care and a synthetic compound applied three times a day, for breakfast, lunch and dinner

(recorded laughter)

our worker's offspring grew wings and subsequently became queens, ready to fly to mate and establish a new colony. We allowed them to reproduce and we are now keeping under observation four queens who successfully started a colony. As not everybody here is an expert in ants, I am not going to give you all the dirty details,

(recorded laughter)

we will be doing that in the focus group tomorrow.

All I can say now is that it feels pretty good to be able to produce a little revolution in the ants' world and turn workers into queens.

Our ants don't attack each other any more, their values are sisterhood, cooperation and personal fulfillment. And they get along remarkably well even with the male-ants now!

(recorded laughter)

Well, of course, that's my personal utopia, but there must be a chemical compound that sorts that out too. We'll work on that!

(recorded laughter)

I already took a lot of your precious time. I, Adam and *(she puts her hands on her belly)* our little Pupa

(recorded laughter)

thank you for your attention and we wish you a great royal weekend.

(recorded applauses – and hopefully real ones too :)

End of Play